THE TRUTH ABOUT CATS
Feline Facts & Folklore

Philip Ardagh writes both fiction and
non-fiction, and is a familiar face at book
festivals in England, Scotland and Wales.
His books have been translated into
numerous languages, including Latin.

THE TRUTH ABOUT CATS

Feline Facts & Folklore

Philip Ardagh

Illustrated by Caroline Smith

MACMILLAN

For Beanie and Snorkel, gone from our lives,
but in my heart forever.

First published 2006 by Macmillan Children's Books
a division of Macmillan Publishers Ltd
20 New Wharf Road, London N1 9RR
Basingstoke and Oxford
www.macmillan.com

Associated companies throughout the world

ISBN-13: 978-1-4050-6710-2
ISBN-10: 1-4050-6710-1

1 3 5 7 9 8 6 4 2

A CIP catalogue record for this book is available
from the British Library.

Printed in China

Contents

Nine Lives

Cats are said to have nine lives. Nine has always been a mystical number, consisting of a trinity of trinity (in other words, three threes). According to the ancient Greeks, this made the number the perfect plural. It certainly keeps on cropping up in their mythology, from the nine heads of the terrifying Hydra to Vulcan, the god of fire, taking nine days to fall from the gods' home on Olympus to earth. In Norse mythology, there were nine worlds in hell, and the chief Norse god Odin's magic golden ring wept eight other gold rings – making a total of nine – every ninth night.

Folklore

In folklore, many chants need to be spoken nine times to have the desired effect, or nine specific items need to be gathered or created. A piece of black wool with nine knots in it, for example, is said to be the cure for a sprained ankle, if worn around it. Seeing nine magpies was thought to be very unlucky indeed. Nine is also, of course, the number of months of a human pregnancy, so this adds further importance to the number when used in charms and divinations.

Survivors

So how did cats come to be said to have so many lives? The initial answer probably lies in their agility. Cats can run up curtains, leap almost vertically, walk along the top of the thinnest of fences, squeeze through the tiniest of openings and, when they fall, they invariably land on their paws. In other words, they survive numerous scrapes which would probably have killed another animal. So, saying cats have nine lives is another way of saying they're lucky.

Choosing the mystical number nine adds symbolism and magic to their feats of survival and, as you'll see throughout this book, cats have always been associated with luck – both good and bad – and, of course, with magic.

Black Cats

Even today, black cats are associated with witches in books, films, TV shows and the common psyche. The big difference nowadays is that far fewer people get victimized, let alone killed, for being a witch.

Although black cats were seen as being witches' familiars – evil spirits or demons in animal form – they were, in fact, only one of many animals used as an excuse to accuse women of witchcraft. In mainland Europe, there was the dreadful midsummer practice of burning 'satanic cats' on bonfires in the sixteenth and seventeenth centuries.

Shapeshifting

As well as supposedly having them around to assist with their magic – though toads, rabbits and pigs, among others, were also said to be familiars, fulfilling the same function – some so-called witches were also thought to have the ability to change into black cats. This is the lasting image which survives today – possibly because black cats blend so expertly into the darkness of the night, and their eyes can look so startling in the blackness – but there are, in truth, far more reports of witches becoming hares.

Good luck/bad luck

With such a strong association with evil witches, it's hardly surprising that black cats are considered, by many, to be bad luck. A black cat crossing your path is even worse than walking under a ladder. It is surprising, then, that in England today most people consider black cats good luck. They even appear on greetings cards and as good-luck charms.

There are other examples of black being a lucky colour: soot-covered chimney sweeps were considered good luck, as is the piece of coal traditionally given in the custom of 'first footing'. First footing is where, to bring a home a year's good luck, the first person entering the house on New Year's Day (just after midnight on New Year's Eve) brings in a piece of coal and often, bread and salt. Interestingly, in many places, it was also important that the first footer – the first person to cross the threshold that year – be dark-skinned or dark-haired. Now limited mainly to Scotland in the UK, this used to be a widespread custom in England too.

One other example of a black animal seen by some as good and others as bad is the black sheep. A single black lamb in a flock was seen as good. Being described as 'the black sheep of the family', however, is not a compliment!

Letting the Cat Out of the Bag

If you don't want someone to give the game away – let slip a secret – then the common cry is, 'Don't let the cat out of the bag!' We all know what it means, but not necessarily why it means it. After all, a cat isn't a secret, surely?

The answer lies in another, now less commonly used, saying: 'Never buy a pig in a poke', meaning that you should know what you're letting yourself in for. This saying comes from an old trick used on the unwary at market: the conman sells you a sack (called a poke) with what he claims is a suckling pig inside it.

It's only when you've parted with your hard-earned cash and opened the bag that you discover that it's not a pig at all, but a 'valueless' cat! By letting the cat out of the bag, the secret is revealed.

The Cat's Pyjamas or
the Cat's Whiskers

Two familiar phrases concerning cats have the same meaning. Both 'the cat's pyjamas' and 'the cat's whiskers' refer to something attractive and first rate. (Both phrases are also used negatively, as in 'He thinks he's the cat's pyjamas', implying that, whoever he is, he isn't!) The phrase originated in America in the 1900s (probably in girls' schools) but was all the rage in England in the roaring 1920s and 1930s.

A cat's whisker also referred to the incredibly thin wire that made contact with the crystal in one of the very earliest forms of radio: the crystal wireless set.

'He has gone to fish, for his Aunt Jobiska's
Runcible Cat with crimson whiskers!'

From 'The Pobble Who Has No Toes'
– Edward Lear (1812–88)

Silent Footfalls

Cats walk silently on padded paws but, according to Norse mythology, it didn't always used to be this way. The sound of cats' footfalls was one of the magic ingredients that was needed to create the rope Gleipnir, which was used to restrain the giant wolf Fenris until the battle at the end of time.

Along with the sound of cats' footfalls, women's beards, mountains' roots, fishes' voices and birds' spittle were also used which, apparently, is why these things don't exist today!

Thor and the Cat
on the Hearth

Another cat in Norse mythology was the one in the king's castle in Utgard, land of the giants. The giant king challenged Thor, the god of thunder, and his companions to a series of tasks and defeated them through trickery: Thor tried to drink a horn of water, unaware that it was attached to the oceans (and he drank so much he created the tides); Thialfi raced Hugi, only to discover that Hugi was Thought itself, and nothing is faster than a thought; Loki was defeated in an eating competition by Fire, and nothing is hungrier than fire; and Thor was defeated in a wrestling competition by the king's nursemaid, Elli. He started off well, but eventually she overpowered him. This was hardly surprising, as Elli turned out to be Old Age, and she defeats us all in the end.

Which left the ordinary-sized cat sleeping by the fire. It wasn't even a giant one. Lift that, and Thor would earn the respect of all in Utgard. He tried. He failed. Once again he'd been tricked. The cat was really the magically transformed Jormungand, a serpent so large that it circled the whole earth and bit its own tail. Defeated, Thor and his party left the castle, but only after the king had told him how he'd been duped.

Dick Whittington's Cat

That Dick Whittington of pantomime fame was a real person is not in dispute. He was Sir Richard Whittington, Lord Mayor of London on three separate occasions between 1397 and 1420. He was also the richest merchant of the day.

Legend has it that he and his cat came to London to seek his fortune, and that he was on the verge of giving up when he heard the Bow bells peeling out a message to him:

Turn Back Dick Whittington,
Thrice Lord Mayor of London.

So Dick did turn back and, purely by chance, he then ended up selling his cat, at a great price, to the King of Barbary, whose kingdom was overrun with rats and mice!

What type of cat is this?

The great thing about this story is that the cat in question may not have started out as the feline – miaow-miaow, purr-purr – variety at all. One theory is that it was in fact a type of flat-bottomed ship the real Whittington used to transport coal to London. Another is based on the fact that the French word *achat*, which means 'purchase', was commonly used to mean 'trading at a profit' in medieval England . . . and *chat* is the French for cat. You can see how the confusion might have arisen.

Butter their Paws!

A common fear when moving to a new house is that the pet cat will try to find its way back to the old one (just think of Tao, the Siamese cat in *The Incredible Journey*). One suggested solution is putting butter on their paws. The theory is that, once they've licked every last trace of lovely butter off their paws and from between their claws, they'll have forgotten all thoughts of roaming . . . and may even be hoping for another buttering the following day!

Ancient Egyptians and their Cats

Ancient Egyptians were crazy about cats. The Greek historian Herodotus, who studied life in ancient Egypt, was amazed to find that, when a house caught fire, its occupants and neighbours were far more interested in saving the cats than putting the fire out. (Obviously ancient Greeks weren't as sentimental about their own pets!) However, deliberately killing a cat in ancient Egypt was a crime punishable by death . . . so cat rescue was probably the wisest form of action anyway.

Pampered pets

Egyptians kept everything from dogs to snakes and monkeys but, though less popular than dogs, cats held a very special place in their hearts. When a pet cat died, it was the owner's custom to shave off his own eyebrows in mourning.

The goddess Bast

As well as having cats for pets, the ancient Egyptians worshipped them, and one in particular: the goddess Bast (also known as Bas and Bastet). Each Egyptian god was believed to inhabit the earth in a sacred animal form: Horus as a falcon, for example. Bast prowled the earth in the form of a cat. A live cat was always kept in each

The Truth About Cats

temple dedicated to her and, when it died, it was mummified and buried in a special cemetery, and a new cat put in the temple in its place.

Mummified moggies

Incredibly, in the early twentieth century, around 300,000 mummified cats were shipped over from Egypt to England and turned into fertilizer! Insensitive though this may sound, tomb robbing was actually an even bigger problem in ancient Egyptian times than later on. By the time Tutankhamun was on the throne of Egypt, every single pyramid had been robbed of the treasures buried with the dead royalty inside it.

Hathor the lioness

Though usually in the form of a placid cow when on the Earth, the goddess Hathor once nearly destroyed humankind while in the form of one of the most ferocious big cats – a lioness – or so ancient Egyptian mythology has it. According to the story, her father, Ra, the mighty sun god, was tired of the humans he had created showing him no respect, so he ordered her to kill them all.

Later he regretted his decision, but did not know how he could stop her now she had tasted blood and was on the rampage. And, anyway, he couldn't be seen going back on his own word. That might make him seem weak.

His solution was ingenious and worthy of the king of the gods. He had seven thousand jars of barley beer mixed with red earth (called ochre) so that it looked like blood. Hathor the lioness lapped it all up, became drunk and drowsy and wanted to sleep. All thoughts of violence left her. She returned to her father's palace, and the human race was saved.

(When the Nile floods, its waters sometimes

turn red when mixed with the red soil. Could this be a reminder of Ra's solution, or what inspired the story in the first place? Who knows.)

The Cheshire Cat

There are those who claim that the phrase 'to grin like a Cheshire cat' predates the animal's appearance in *Alice's Adventures in Wonderland*, and those who claim that it came from the book. Either way, there's no disputing that it is Lewis Carroll's book which made the creature famous, along with the picture of him by Tenniel. Of course, cats don't grin. If they bare their teeth, it's not to express happiness!

No one seems to know exactly where the idea for a grinning Cheshire cat comes from. Cheshire is famous for its cheese, and there are claims that it used to be sold in the shape of a grinning cat. (To add to the confusion, nowadays, photographers often ask you to 'say cheese!' when they want you to grin for a picture.)

> *The Cat only grinned when it saw Alice. It looked good-natured, she thought: still it had very long claws and a great many teeth, so she felt that it ought to be treated with respect.*

From *Alice's Adventures in Wonderland*
– Lewis Carroll (1832–98)

Catgut Tennis Rackets

Not that long ago – certainly when I was a child, and I'm not that ancient – tennis rackets were made out of catgut. I was horrified when I learned this, and couldn't understand why some rackets proudly proclaimed 'genuine catgut' on their wooden handles. The good news is that catgut isn't actually the dried and twisted intestines of cats. The bad news is that it's the dried intestines of sheep or horses. Anyone for tennis?

Thomas Hardy's Heart

It was the famous English novelist and poet Thomas Hardy's wish that, when he died, he be buried in the churchyard at Stinsford in Dorset but, when it came to it in 1928, the British government wanted him buried in Westminster Abbey. Hardy's widow and Stanley Baldwin's government came to an agreement: Hardy's body would be interred in Westminster Abbey (along with those of many of the literary giants of England), but his heart would be buried in the Wessex he loved so much. This is not disputed. It is here on in that the versions of events differ.

One version is straightforward enough: Hardy's heart was removed, stored overnight and buried the following day. The other two versions involve cats.

The doctor's cat

Hardy's family physician refused to remove the heart, so one of his assistants, who was willing to earn his place in history carried out the procedure. But what to do with the heart once it was removed? According to this telling of the tale, his maid put it in a biscuit tin for safekeeping. . . but not safe enough. In the night, his cat found the heart and ate it!

The sister's cat

The third version has Hardy's sister's cat eating

the heart, left for a moment by the late-Hardy's housekeeper on the kitchen table.

A heartless end

While there's no disputing that Hardy's body was given a funeral with national honours, rumours still abound as to what was buried in the churchyard in Stinsford. It could simply have been his heart, as planned. Another suggestion is that, following a cat having eaten it, a pig's heart – from the local butcher's shop, one assumes – was buried in its place. Most sinister of all is the claim that the cat that had eaten the heart was killed and buried on the spot so that, in a sense, the heart (though digested) was in its rightful place. Perhaps we'll never know, but as well as being a gruesome tale it's also an intriguing one.

The Cat and Fiddle

The Cat and Fiddle used to be a popular pub name in Britain. There's even one called that in the fictitious village of Ambridge in BBC Radio 4's *The Archers* (the other pub being the Bull). The most likely derivation of the name comes from one of the games that landlords used to provide for their patrons, tipcat (also known as trapball). There would also be a fiddler for the drinkers to dance to. In other words, the name of the pub was proclaiming what the inn had to offer as well as drink.

Tipcat involved getting a ball into a cup on a stick. (The name could have come from the string of catgut joining the stick and ball together.)

This is another example of a non-feline cat turning into one over time (see page 16).

Hey diddle diddle,
The cat and the fiddle,
The cow jumped over the moon,
The little dog laughed
To see such fun,
And the dish ran away
With the spoon.

– Traditional English rhyme

Puss in Boots

The one cat as famous as Dick Whittington's, if not more so, is Puss in Boots, who helped pass off his master (a young miller) as 'the Marquis of Carabas' and secured him a fortune and a beautiful wife . . . Not in real life, of course. The first recorded version of this nursery tale appeared, in Italian, in *Straparola's Nights* in 1530. It was translated into French in 1585 and the story finally reached England in a French collection of tales published in 1697.

Pussy Cat, Pussy Cat

Have you ever stopped to wonder why a cat is sometimes referred to as a puss, pussy, or pussy cat? The most popular theory seems to be that the word 'puss' is a cat-like sound. You can also see how calling a cat quietly, at night for example, could easily turn from 'pssst!' to 'puss!'. The whole issue is somewhat confused by the fact that, by the seventeenth century, the name puss was also applied to hares . . . but this is probably because the Latin for hare is *lepus*!

Cats and the Weather

There were people who believed that you could predict the weather by watching a cat's behaviour, and others who thought that the cat was actually creating the weather conditions.

Raining cats and dogs

The phrase 'raining cats and dogs' isn't as random or ridiculous as it might at first sound. In Norse mythology, cats had plenty to do with affecting the weather, and dogs – attendants of the chief god Odin himself – were closely associated with the wind. So, put a cat and a dog together and you should end up with a plentiful supply of wind and rain: quite a downpour, in fact. The Quechua Indians of South America believe that the evil cat spirit Ccoa is responsible for killer hail and lightning (see pages 50–51).

The cat forecast

There's an old sailors' saying, on seeing a frisky cat, 'The cat has a gale of a wind in her tail.' But Jonathan Swift (possibly most famous for having written *Gulliver's Travels*) seems to have had the opposite belief. He wrote that, when rain is on the way: 'the pensive cat gives o'er/Her frolics, and pursues her tail no more'.

Facing the wind

It was observed long ago that cats face into the

wind when washing, but this wasn't necessarily seen as an omen of anything. When a cat washes its face, however, it's thought to be a sign of rain . . . or of sunshine . . . or that someone's about to pay you a visit. You see the problem?

To calm the storm

In Ireland, it was once common practice to put a frisky cat under an upturned cooking pot – in much the same way one might capture a spider under a glass – in the hope that it would calm down and, as a result, the storm outside would calm down too . . . which is the exact opposite of the mariner's saying that a troublemaker can cause a storm by putting a cat under a pot.

Other cat forecasts

In Indonesia, the Malay people have an old

tradition that a bathing cat will cause rain, while Welsh tradition has it that a constantly miaowing ship's cat portends a rough sea voyage ahead, and a playful cat means that they should – very specifically – expect a gale astern (from the direction of the back of the ship).

Witches' tricks

Witches were said to ride on storms in cat form, or to use their cat familiars to bring about bad weather. In the famous trial of the Scottish 'witch' Agnes Sampson, in the sixteenth century, she claimed responsibility for raising a storm with the intention of wrecking the ship carrying King James and his Danish wife, Queen Anne, from Scotland to Denmark, and said that she'd used a cat to do it.

Cats' Eyes

It's long been a tradition in many parts of the world, from China to the USA, that you can tell the time of day by looking at a cat's eyes. You can see how the idea arose. It's based on logical observation that when it's dark – early in the morning or in the evening, say – the cat needs to let as much light into its eyes as possible, so the hole in the middle of the eye (the pupil) needs to open wide. When it's very bright out – in the height of the midday sun, for example – the eye needs to restrict the amount of light getting into it, so the hole becomes that familiar cat's-eye slit (an elliptical pupil).

The eyes have it

In some parts of the world, though, there's the rather less scientific folklore that the pupils in a cat's eyes are tiny at low tide, and wide open and huge at high tide. And even more outlandish is the ancient British belief that staring into a cat's eyes was like staring through a window into the world of spirits.

Catseyes in the road

Today, many people think of 'cats' eyes' as the special reflective studs in a protective casing embedded in the road surface, designed to reflect light from car headlights back at the driver so they don't lose their bearings in the dark. These catseyes (actually spelled as one word, without an apostrophe) were invented by English businessman Percy Shaw in the 1930s. The first catseyes were installed on a stretch of new road in Bradford in Yorkshire in 1934. This simple but brilliant idea eventually made him a very rich man indeed.

Shaw claimed that he'd got the idea for catseyes from reflectors attached to a roadside poster, and from a cat he'd seen sitting on a wall reflecting the light back from its eyes.

On reflection

Cats are said to see at least six times better than we humans can in the dark, and seeing the light reflected from their eyes, as Shaw did, helps to explain why. Just behind the retina, cats' eyes have a layer of mirror-like cells, called the *tapetum lucidum*, which reflects all available light back into the retina to maximize vision in even the faintest light. Cats also have amazing peripheral vision. In other words, they can see what's happening for a whole 285 degrees or so around them. This is useful when hunting . . . or being hunted.

Quite a spectacle

It has been pointed out, however, that if cats could read, they'd probably need to wear glasses or, in this day and age, contact lenses! Their close vision isn't that good, because being able to see something right in front of your nose isn't as useful as seeing hunter or prey when you're a cat in the wild.

Some cats may enjoy watching television – and even get interactive, batting the screen with their paw – but they don't see what we see. What appears to us as solid blocks of colour, appears to a cat as flickering light.

Eye colour and deafness

Most cats are born with blue eyes but, usually between twelve weeks and six months, their true colour emerges. In the case of cats with white fur, the majority of those with blue eyes are deaf. Even more strangely, in the instances where white cats have just one blue eye (and the other is, say, orange), only the ear on the same side as that eye is deaf!

Do you see what I see?

It's not true that cats see everything in black and white. In the same way that most colour-blind people have a blindness to certain colours (and/or the combinations those colours create), cats have more of a colour deficiency. They can't see red.

Blind at birth

Like many mammals, cats are born blind. Without

41

sight, tiny kittens get to know their immediate surroundings with their noses. They use the touch receptors in them to make contact with their mother and siblings, which is why nose-to-nose contact with other cats, in later life, is a friendly greeting. (And why you should feel honoured when a cat touches its nose to yours, too.) A cat's nosepad – the part without fur – is believed to be as unique to every cat as fingerprints are to us humans.

A Clowder of Cats

The collective noun for a group of domestic cats is a clowder. We're all familiar with a pride of lions, a school of whales, a flock of sheep and a swarm of bees, but other – more unusual – collective nouns include: a crash of rhinos, a parliament of owls, a murder of crows and (my favourite) a smuck of jellyfish! A clowder refers only to a group of adult domestic cats. A group of kittens is a kindle!

The Cat's Only Trick

There is an old, old story about a cat and a fox that is well known right across Europe, a version of which appears in *Aesop's Fables* (originally collected together in written form in about 300 BC).

The story tells of how a fox is bragging that, whatever the danger, he has a hundred tricks with which to save himself, whereas the cat has only one . . . and not a very impressive one at that. All she can do is run up a tree. He, on the other hand, can use cunning and stealth and . . . and at that moment

44

a pack of hounds appears. The cat simply uses her one and only trick. She dashes up a tree to safety. From there she watches the fox try every one of his hundred tricks and fail. The hounds catch him.

The moral? That the simple approach is sometimes the best, perhaps? Or who needs lots of tricks when a tried and tested method works well? Or maybe it simply goes to show just how smart cats really are!

Belling the Cat

Another of *Aesop's Fables* (see pages 44–5), concerns a gathering of mice at a meeting especially convened to try to come up with ways of ridding themselves of the cat who is making their lives a misery.

After some discussion, one young mouse comes up with a seemingly excellent suggestion: if they were to tie a bell around the cat's neck, then they'd be able to hear when it was coming and, so, run and hide. All the other mice think that this is a great idea, until a wise old mouse steps into the centre of the circle. 'There's just one thing,' he says. 'Who will put the bell on the cat?'

The term 'belling the cat' has, therefore, come to mean any proposed solution to a problem that sounds good on the surface, but doesn't stand up to scrutiny . . . or any remedy that's impossible to actually implement.

Ai Apaec

On the northern coast of Peru, the supreme god of gods of the Mochica people was Ai Apaec, who had part feline and part human form. He was most often seen as a wrinkled old man but with cat's fangs and whiskers, though he's sometimes shown with a human face on one side of his head and a cat's face – still with human eyes – on the other. Ai Apaec was kind-natured and powerful. A musician, farmer, healer and fisherman, he was also a mighty fighter, defeating everything from demons and dragons to vampires.

He was served by a lizard, and his best friend and counsellor was a dog.

Ccoa, the Peruvian Cat Spirit

The Quechua Indians of South America believe – or used to believe – that each mountain peak in the Peruvian Andes was inhabited by spirits called aukis and one of the servants of the aukis is Ccoa, the evil cat spirit. Whether simply following orders or acting on his own initiative, Ccoa causes humans a great deal of trouble.

Said to be storm-grey and stripy, his most striking feature is not his foot-long tail or even his phosphorescent eyes but the hail streaming from his

50

eyes and ears. Ccoa is the cause of hail and lightning, which he often uses as a weapon to harm people or to cause damage.

Sorcerers derive their magical power from him so are his devoted servants and do his bidding. Quick to anger, Ccoa must be continually supplied with magical offerings to soothe his rage.

The King of the Cats

One of the most enduring of cat myths, legends and folklore is that there is a King of the Cats, and variations of this tale have been told time and time again. A common version is the tale within a tale. A man is telling a friend of the extraordinary sight he's seen – an elaborate funeral for a cat, of all things – when the man's own cat, who has been sitting on the hearth – ears twitching and one eye open – suddenly cries, 'So now I'm the King of the Cats!' and leaps to his feet and up the chimney, never to be seen again.

Royal revenge

A less pleasant version hails from Ireland. A man killed a cat but, before it died, it said, 'When you go home, let them know you've killed the King of the Cats.' When the man got home, he did just that only to have his own cat leap up and kill him with tooth and claw.

A poet's folly

Another Irish legend has it that Irusan was King of the Cats. Living in a cave at Knowth in County Meath, he was said to be as big as an ox. Once, he was insulted by a poem recited by the poet Senchan, so he snatched him up and made off with him. When passing through Clonmacnoise, however, Irusan was killed by a red-hot bar thrown by St Ciaran, who had built a church there, and the poet was rescued.

Cats in May

I used to live in the county of Sussex, where there's an old belief that a kitten born in the month of May will grow up to be a melancholy cat. In many parts of rural England, there's also the tradition that 'a May cat will never make a mouser'. The belief is even more specific than that. It goes on to say that a May cat is far more likely to bring home snakes or glow-worms than kill mice! There is a suggestion that they should be drowned, but counter-wisdom suggests that such an action – quite apart from being cruel by modern standards, of course – could bring bad luck.

> *The rats by night such mischief did,*
> *Betty was every morning chid.*
> *They undermined whole sides of bacon,*
> *Her cheese was sapp'd, her tarts were taken.*
> *Her pasties, fenced with thickest paste,*
> *Were all demolish'd, and laid waste.*
> *She cursed the Cat for want of duty,*
> *Who left her foes a constant booty.*

From 'The Rat-Catcher and Cats'
– John Gay (1685–1732)

Stealing a Sleeper's Breath

A very common piece of folklore is that you should never let a cat near a baby in its cot. This is sound advice if you're worried about the child inhaling cat hair, or that the cat may weigh heavily on the baby's chest or somehow smother it. Cats do like warm places to snuggle down! The old fear, however, was that the cat would put its own mouth near the baby's and steal its breath – sucking the life from its body.

The Beast of Bodmin

In the 1990s, there were reported sightings of a big cat – perhaps even a puma – on Bodmin Moor in Cornwall, and the mysterious creature was quickly dubbed 'The Beast of Bodmin' in the press. Interestingly, this is only one example of many reports of out-sized cats in unlikely locations. (There was the 'Black Beast of Exmoor' in 1983, for example.) Theories range from abandoned or escaped exotic pets, circus or zoo animals; tricks of perspective making a big fat moggy appear to be even larger still; pranksters; a breed of long-forgotten big cats still living wild, or even some form of alien intervention. In each instance, most evidence is anecdotal. Little physical evidence turns up by comparison.

Thou makest darkness that it may be night:
wherein all the beasts of the forest do move.

From Psalm 104
– King James's Bible

On the Move

Cats move in an unusual way for four-legged animals. There are only two other animals that employ a similar technique: the camel and the giraffe, neither of which seems very catlike!

Cats first move the front and back legs on one side of their body, then the front and back legs on the other (rather than using both front legs first and then the back ones, as a dog does, for example). This is what gives cats their very distinctive lolloping walk and bouncy side-to-side stride.

On their toes

Cats walk on their toes (with the back part of the foot raised), a method known as digitigrade. A person who tiptoes around a matter, rather than getting stuck in, is sometimes accused of 'pussyfooting around'.

The average domestic cat has five toes on each front paw and four toes on each back paw. Those born with extra toes are said to be polydactyl. Jake, an orange tabby cat from Ontario, Canada, holds the Guinness World Record for the cat with the most toes: twenty-eight in total!

Left or right?

In the same way that most of us are either left-handed or right-handed as opposed to ambidextrous (which means one doesn't favour one hand over the other), around sixty per cent of cats favour either their left or right paw for dipping in water, bobbing balls about the room and so on! The remaining forty per cent use either. A cat's paws are sensitive to the slightest touch and are believed to be able to pick up tiny vibrations.

But the Kitten, how she starts,
Crouches, stretches, paws and darts!
First at one, and then its fellow;
Just as light and just as yellow;
There are many now – now one –
Now they stop and there are none . . .

From 'The Kitten and the Falling Leaves'
– William Wordsworth (1770–1850)

Flexible Felines

The average domestic cat has many more bones in its body than an adult human's mere 206. A cat's spine not only contains more vertebrae than a human's but these are also less tightly connected, which helps to make the spine – and thus the cat – incredibly flexible. A cat has the ability to compress or stretch its spine as need arises. The smaller the spine, the smaller the spot a cat can curl up and get cosy in. A longer spine, however, means a greater leap. The power of a cat's pounce comes from the size of its thighs in relation to its body. These are mighty powerful muscles! It's a cat's remarkable flexibility that helps it pull off the trick of landing right-side-up (see pages 64–5).

Landing Feet First

Falling cats – whether jumping or having been pushed – go through a 'standard procedure' to get upright before hitting the ground. Firstly, they rotate their head, then they twist their spine so that their back legs are in the landing position. Finally, they arch their back so that it will soften the impact when they hit the ground. All these actions can be carried out in less than a second. Cats do not land upright a hundred per cent of the time, so should never be dropped to put them to the test.

A falling cat rights itself

There is a suggestion that a cat has a better chance of surviving a fall from a twenty-storey window than a seven-storey one, because it takes a fall of about eight storeys for the cat to realize what has happened and to switch into uprighting mode. You do the maths!

Catnapping

Domestic cats get more sleep than most animals. They're consummate professionals at snoozing, averaging sixteen hours a day. (Lions will sleep for twenty hours in the wild, given half the chance.) A domestic cat will spend about seventy per cent of the day sleeping and fifteen per cent grooming, which leaves fifteen per cent of the day to do everything else, including eating! Many people describe cats as sleeping 'with half an ear open'. Even when a cat's asleep, it appears to be listening out for possible danger, its ears swivelling like a radar dish. They sleep in short bursts – catnaps – and are ready to leap into action, fitting the day's activities in-between.

To dream or not to dream?

Judging by REM (Rapid Eye Movement), whisker twitching, tail flicking and paw flexing, scientists believe that cats do, indeed, dream, starting from when they're about a week old.

Hot spots

Cats like to be warmer than we do, which is why they like nothing more than sleeping in front of a fire, right up against a radiator, or even in an airing cupboard.

Catnip

Catnip (*Nepeta cataria*) – also known as catmint – is a small plant with soft, downy leaves and purple or white flowers, which has an amazing effect on about eighty per cent of cats, including the big cats, such as lions or tigers. Size doesn't matter: catnip can drive them wild. Most cats love the smell of catnip: it makes them playful and happy. Many toys for cats contain catnip, and a catnip-filled toy mouse is often a firm favourite with cats. Having said that, of the eighty per cent of cats who react to the plant, they do react in varying degrees. While some go crazy for it, others display more of a take-it-or-leave-it attitude.

Kitty-corner

The term kitty-corner – most popular in the US, and meaning facing diagonally opposite – is a prime example of a phrase which suggests that it's something to do with cats, when it isn't. The term started out as cater-corner in the nineteenth century, a corruption of the French word *quatre* meaning four (going all the way back to the Latin *quattuor*). Soon cater metamorphosed into the word kitty . . . so people are left wondering what sitting diagonally opposite someone has to do with kittens!

Cat Doors

Today, cat flaps are a familiar sight, enabling cats to go in and out of the house as they please, but one of the earliest records of a cat door was of one made by Sir Isaac Newton in the seventeenth century. Better known for discovering gravity – after supposedly watching an apple fall – Sir Isaac was also devoted to his cat. He had a hole cut in the bottom of an outside door at Woolsthorpe Manor for her to use. When the cat had kittens, he had an additional kitten-sized hole cut next to it, for their personal use!

Cats in the White House

There have been many famous cats in the White House, one of the more recent ones being Socks, belonging to President Bill Clinton's family. Earlier feline occupants included Theodore Roosevelt's cat, Tom Quartz, about whom a biography was published.

The cat that got the cream

There's an oft-told tale of a visitor to the White House breakfasting with President Calvin Coolidge. Part way through the meal, the president poured some milk into his saucer. Not wanting to be thought ignorant of some strange White House etiquette, the guest copied him . . . only to see Coolidge bend down and place the saucer on the floor by his feet. A cat appeared from under the table and began lapping the milk. The president smiled, the guest's face reddened, and the cat purred contentedly.

Tom Kitten and the Kennedys

Tom Kitten moved into the White House with President Kennedy and his family, and was instantly the darling of the Washington press. He was even quoted in newspapers! He wasn't a fan of all the comings and goings of the politicians, statesmen and staff, and moved to Alexandria, Virginia, to live with Jackie Kennedy's secretary. Tom Kitten died in 1962. His obituary in Alexandria's *Gazette* included these tongue-in-cheek words:

73

Unlike many humans in the same position, he never wrote his memoirs of his days in the White House . . . though he was privy to many official secrets.

The following year, President Kennedy was assassinated.

Acater, the Loyal Cat

In the late fifteenth century, the English were divided between those who supported the House of York and those who supported the House of Lancaster. When the Duke of York became King Richard III, those loyal to Lancaster were in for a tough time. One such person was Sir Henry Wyatt, who was imprisoned in the Tower of London, where he was tortured and starved. Conditions in the jail were atrocious and legend has it that Sir Henry would probably have died if he hadn't been befriended by a cat, called variously Acater or Accator.

Food and warmth

Everyday, Acater would squeeze through the bars of the window of Sir Henry's prison cell with a freshly killed 'pigeon' – probably from a nearby dovecote – in his jaws (which a sympathetic jailer cooked for the prisoner). At night, the cat snuggled up with Sir Henry, giving him company and warmth.

Loyalty rewarded

When Richard III was killed at the Battle of Bosworth Field in 1485, Sir Henry was freed by the new king, Henry VII. But Sir Henry Wyatt never forgot Acater's role in his survival. The legend ends by saying that he had a fine monument built to his loyal feline friend in a churchyard in Boxley in Kent, now long gone.

True or not?

There's no denying that poor Sir Henry went through all the horrors outlined, but there are no contemporary reports of the role played by a cat. There are, however, two portraits of Sir Henry with a cat, and records state that he showed as much interest in cats as other men, more normally, showed in hounds. Sir Henry went on to become guardian to the king's son and, later, Master of the King's Jewels and Treasurer of the King's Chamber.

What's in a name?

As well as being the name of Sir Henry's legendary feline saviour, *acater* is the old Norman French for 'to buy', from which the word cater and caterer is derived . . . and he certainly provided the imprisoned Sir Henry with an excellent catering service!

'A Very Fine Cat Indeed'

Dr Samuel Johnson is most famous for two things: his dictionary, and his life as described by his biographer, James Boswell. In his dictionary, Johnson described a cat as being 'a domestic animal that catches mice, commonly reckoned by naturalists [as] the lowest order of the leonine species'. That may be what naturalists reckoned, but not necessarily Johnson himself. He was a real ailurophile (cat lover).

Boswell wasn't such a cat fan, describing himself as having 'an antipathy to cats', and wrote about

Johnson's pampering of one particular cat called Hodge. He tells of how Johnson went out and bought him oysters personally, rather than instructing the servants to do so, 'lest the servants having that trouble should take a dislike to the poor creature' (who was probably better fed than they were).

Boswell recalled Hodge 'one day scrambling up Dr Johnson's breast, apparently with much satisfaction, while my friend, smiling and half-whistling, rubbed down his back and pulled him by the tail: and when I observed he was a fine cat, said, "Why, yes, sir, but I have had cats whom I liked better than this"; and then, as if perceiving Hodge to be out of countenance, added, "but this is a very fine cat, a very fine cat indeed."'

Faith, the Blitz Cat

In honouring an animal for endurance or bravery, we are not only honouring that particular animal for the particular trials it went through, but are also honouring the countless other animals who went through equally harrowing experiences, and the people who lived and worked alongside them.

A cat called Faith

In 1936, a stray cat made herself at home in

the rectory of the church of St Augustine and St Faith in Watling Street, London, having been shooed out of the church itself on more than one occasion. Henry Ross, the rector, decided to call her Faith, and she became a firm favourite with his congregation, coming with him into the pulpit when he preached. In 1939, war was declared, and in August 1940, Faith gave birth to a single kitten: a tom called Panda. On 6 September, Faith suddenly decided she wanted to take Panda to a corner in the basement and, whenever the rector brought him back upstairs, she took him straight back down again.

Death from the skies

The following evening, there was a terrible air raid in which bombs killed more than 400 people. On 9 September – with Henry Ross away on business and then spending the night in a public air-raid

81

shelter – the church and rectory were destroyed in yet another raid. All that remained above ground was the tower. The following morning, he searched the rubble and found Faith and Panda alive, in their little corner of the basement. This seemed like a small miracle after such terrible death and destruction.

For valour

In 1945, with the war at an end, Faith was presented with a special medal for bravery by the PDSA. The People's Dispensary for Sick Animals was founded by Maria Dickin, and the Dickin Medal is the highest award given to animals in the armed forces or civil defence. Because Faith was in neither, Maria Dickin awarded her with a special silver medal. Guests at the ceremony included Ms Dickin herself and the Archbishop of Canterbury. Faith died on 28 September 1948.

Awarded the Highest Honour

To date, the only cat to have been awarded the PDSA Dickin Medal for gallantry (see page 82), is Simon, the ship's cat from the HMS *Amethyst*. In April 1949, the *Amethyst* was ordered up China's famous Yangtze River to relieve HMS *Consort*, which was protecting the British Embassy in Nanking, during the war between the Communist and Nationalist Chinese. Britain remained neutral in the Chinese civil war but the *Amethyst* was fired on, causing it to run aground on a mudbank.

Death and injury

Twenty-five members of the crew died as a result of the attack, including the captain. Simon had his whiskers and eyebrows singed off, and shrapnel in his leg and back. Remarkably, he made an excellent recovery and attended the funeral service, where the dead sailors' bodies were committed to the water. The plucky black-and-white cat was soon back on rat-catching duty, and visiting the sailors in the sick bay.

Free at last

In July 1949, after 101 days trapped by the enemy, the *Amethyst* managed to get back into open sea, and was sent a telegram of congratulations by King George VI. In August 1949, in a special ceremony, Simon the ship's cat was presented with the campaign ribbon – to which all the crew were entitled – and was given the honorary rank of 'able seaman'. News of what became known as 'the Yangtze Incident' reached the British media, and Simon soon became the darling of the press. He was awarded the Dickin Medal for his gallantry and sent a special collar to wear aboard ship.

In recognition

The *Amethyst* arrived back in England on 1 November 1949. Simon was to be presented with the actual medal on 11 December, but, sadly, died of a virus on 28 November – his health weakened by his injuries – so never received it. Fittingly, Simon's funeral was conducted by Henry Ross, rector of St Augustine's and St Faith's church, and closely associated with another very brave cat indeed.

A Few Feline Facts

Here are a few titbits too small to merit a page each, but too tasty not to be contained within the pages of *The Truth About Cats*.

According to the book of *Guinness World Records*, at the time of writing, the world's fattest cat was Himmey, a neutered male tabby from Australia, weighing more than 21kg (46lbs 15oz). He had a 39.37cm (15 inch) neck and a 83.82cm (33 inch) waist! (The largest breed of cat is the ragdoll.)

Possibly the longest-living cat was also a tabby, this time a female named Ma from England. She was put to sleep in 1957, aged 34.

The record for giving birth to the most offspring in her lifetime also goes to a tabby: this time, Dusty from the USA. She was a mother to some 420 kittens!

Ypres has a cat festival every three years on the second Sunday in May, called the Kattenstoet.

Cats use their tails to help them balance. (The domestic cat is the only cat that can raise its tail straight up while walking.)

Cats do not instinctively know how to hunt. Kittens have to be taught by their mothers . . . If they aren't, they can't!

Index